TIME TROOP

THE FUN WAY FOR YOUNG CHILDREN TO LEARN ABOUT THE PAST

Published by the Society for the Understanding of Early Child Development in Scholastics

The Wright Brothers Adventure

Written by Dr. Herodotus
Illustrated by Ken Krekeler

ISBN 0-9762509-1-8

"It's the Time Alarm," said Tina to Tommy and Chronology Dog.

"Come on Time Troop, to the tree house!" exclaimed Chronology Dog.

"I bet Dr. Debunk and his History Hacks are trying to change history again. Let's check the Time Computer," Tommy said as he jumped into the secret tree house.

Beep
Beep

"Oh no!" cried Chronology Dog, "Orville and Wilbur Wright invented and flew the first airplane."

"I've set the time portal," said Tina. "Let's go back in time and stop Dr. Debunk."

"So what if Dr. Debunk stops this one airplane? There are airplanes all over the place," stated Tommy.

"There are lots of airplanes now, Tommy, but back in 1903 there were no airplanes. The Wright brothers, Orville and Wilbur, made the first one that worked," Chronology Dog said, shaking his head.

"You mean if we don't stop Dr. Debunk, the Wright brothers will never fly the first airplane at Kitty Hawk?" Tina gasped.

TIME TROOP TRAVELS BACK IN TIME TO
DECEMBER 17, 1903 - KITTY HAWK, NC

"That's right, Tina. Many of the Wright brothers' ideas are still used today and they are among the world's best known inventors," stated Chronology Dog.

"Don't worry, Chronology," said Tommy with pride. "We'll stop Dr. Debunk and the Wright brothers will fly their airplane."

"Ha, Bedlam, I will stop the Wright brother from making the first flight in an airplane. We will erase their deeds from history!" snorted Dr. Debunk. "You two History Hacks, take the heavy weights to the airplane and make sure you aren't seen by anyone."

"I have sand in my hair, and I don't understand how we can stop an airplane with just two History Hacks and some heavy weights," sighed Bedlam the rat. "Airplanes can pick up hundreds of people at a time."

"You're thinking about modern airplanes, Bedlam. The first airplane that ever flew is right over there. It's very small and can only carry one person."

"Dr. Debunk, do you mean that funny looking thing is an airplane? I thought it was a just a bunch of sticks," said Bedlam the Rat.

"That's right Bedlam." Dr Debunk laughed wickedly. "The Wright brothers' airplane that they fly here at Kitty Hawk is small and can not lift anything very heavy. The History Hacks will hide the heavy weights on the airplane and it will not be able to take off."

"That's brilliant. The airplane will not be able to fly and the Wright brothers will give up. No one will remember them," Bedlam said, jumping up and down happily.

"All I see is that small building and a lot of sand," Tina said sadly.

"Well, Tina," said Chronology Dog, "Kitty Hawk is mostly sand. The flat sand is one reason why the Wright brothers picked it as a good place to fly the first airplane."

"Wait a minute. Look down there, guys," Tommy yelled excitedly. "I think I see someone moving towards the Wright brothers' airplane."

"It's two of Dr. Debunk's History Hacks and they're carrying something," whispered Tina.

"I bet those are weights," Chronology Dog said. "Dr. Debunk's plan must be to make the plane too heavy to take off. If that happens, the Wright brothers may never make their airplane work. They'll lose their place in history."

"What are we going to do?" asked Tommy.

"Use your mirage ray, Tommy," Chronology Dog said, pointing towards a large sand dune. "Make that sand dune look like the airplane and the History Hacks may put the weights in the wrong place."

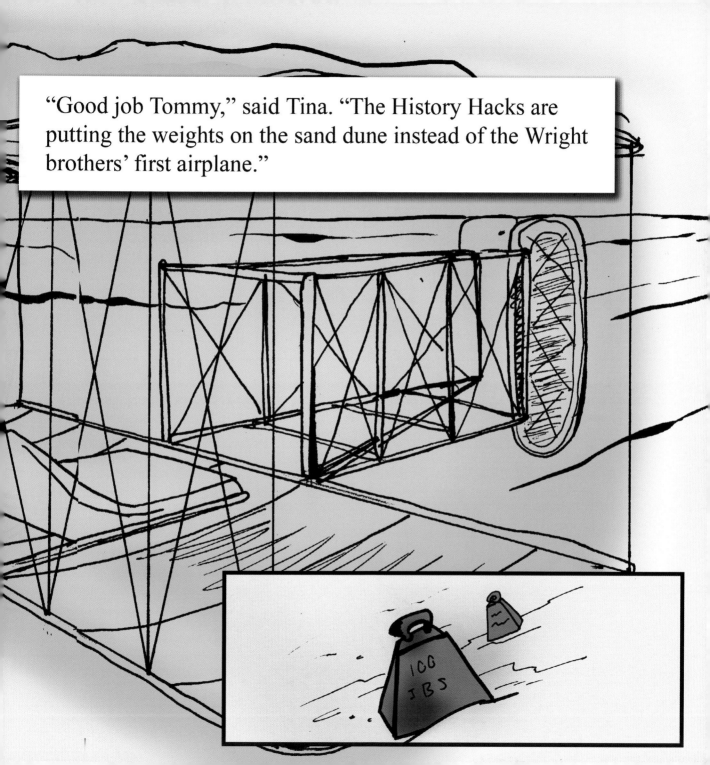

"Good job Tommy," said Tina. "The History Hacks are putting the weights on the sand dune instead of the Wright brothers' first airplane."

"I bet they'll lead us right to Dr. Debunk and Bedlam," Tommy said excitedly.

Chronology Dog pointed towards the sand. "Tina, if you see Dr. Debunk, put the Reset Clock around his neck and send him back to his own time."

"Hey, Dr. Debunk, I thought those two were going to put the weights on the Wright brothers' airplane, not on that sand dune," said Bedlam the Rat.

"What are those History Hacks doing? Can't they follow simple orders?" cried Dr. Debunk. "We have to stop the Wright brothers from being the first people to fly an airplane."

"What?! The Time Troop has stopped us again," Dr. Debunk said as the time portal sends him and the History Hacks back to their own time. "I'll win one of these days."

"Yeah," said Beldam, crying.

"It looks like the Wright brothers managed to fly their airplane, even though it didn't go very far," Tina said to Chronology Dog.

"The Wright brothers' first flight here at Kitty Hawk in 1903 may not have gone very far, but all the large jets people fly in now came from this one small airplane."

"Come on, guys, I want to finish our volleyball game," said Tommy pointing towards the time portal.

Reader, please ask the child/children the following questions:

1. Who invented and flew the first working airplane?
Answer: The Wright brothers.
2. Where did the Wright brothers fly the first airplane?
Answer: Kitty Hawk, North Carolina

The following is a guide to items a child may learn after this book has been read to them several times. Please remember that each child learns differently and this is only a guide.

2 to 5 years old
The first people to invent and fly an airplane were the Wright brothers.
The first airplane flew at Kitty Hawk, North Carolina.

6 and older
The first flight was made on December 17th, 1903.
The plane was light and could not pick up very much weight.
Kitty Hawk was a beach with a lot of sand.
The Wright brothers' first names were Orville and Wilbur.
The flight did not go very high or very far.